The life of
Leonardo da Vinci

WS KIDS
WHITE STAR KIDS

To paint the human form accurately, in all its beauty, it helps to truly understand the inner workings of the body. Not every painter and sculptor has studied anatomy like I have, which is why I will be remembered and admired throughout history for my astonishingly detailed works of art.

I am Leonardo da Vinci and I would love to share with you the story of my life and my work.

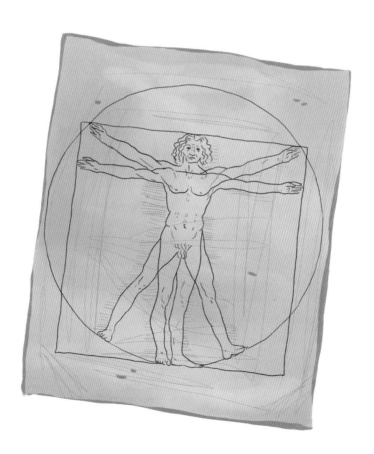

I was born during the Renaissance period, on 15th April 1452. My surname, "da Vinci", simply means "of Vinci", a town in Tuscany close to the place of my birth. My mother, Caterina, was extremely poor, and she and my father never married. So I was brought up by my father, a local notary called Ser Piero, on his family's estate. Beyond some basic reading, writing and mathematics, I didn't get a school education and instead I taught myself.

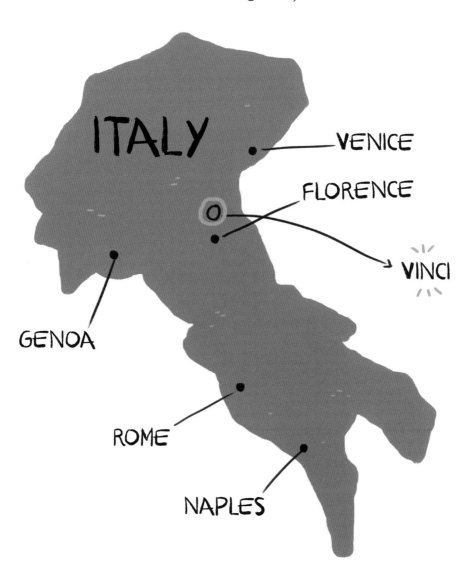

Despite my lack of education, luckily my father spotted that I had a talent for the arts and decided to help me make the most of it. When I was 14, he arranged an apprenticeship for me with Andrea del Verrocchio in Florence. Verrocchio was a well-known sculptor and painter and I was excited to have the opportunity to learn from him.

Whilst studying with Verrocchio I gained a wide range of skills, including metalworking, leather arts, carpentry, drawing, painting and sculpting. I spent many, many years training hard with the master and perfecting my techniques. I often chose to write, draw and paint with my left hand, though I was ambidextrous and equally able to use my right hand.

Finally, in 1478, I had learned all I could from the great Verrocchio. It was now time for me to become an independent master. I got my first commission only a few years later, from the San Donato monastery in Florence. I called the piece "The Adoration of the Magi".

I never did finish that painting, because in about 1483 I moved to Milan and began working for the Sforza family. They were the rulers at that time, and they wanted me to be one of their engineers, architects, painters and sculptors. For over twelve years I worked on a towering bronze equestrian statue to honor the founder of the Sforza dynasty, Francesco Sforza. It would have been magnificent, but when it looked as though there would be a war, the bronze was instead used to make cannons.

Throughout my career I have carried out anatomical studies of the human skeleton, muscles, brain and digestive and reproductive systems. This has given me a new understanding of the human body and has helped enormously with my work. I believe, and always have done, that sight is humankind's most important sense, and therefore the eyes are the most important organ.

I combined this interest in both art and science in around 1490 when I sketched the figure of a man with arms outstretched in two positions, one over the top of the other. It was a study of the relationship between human proportions and geometry - I got the idea from the Roman architect Vitruvius, so the drawing is known as "Vitruvian Man".

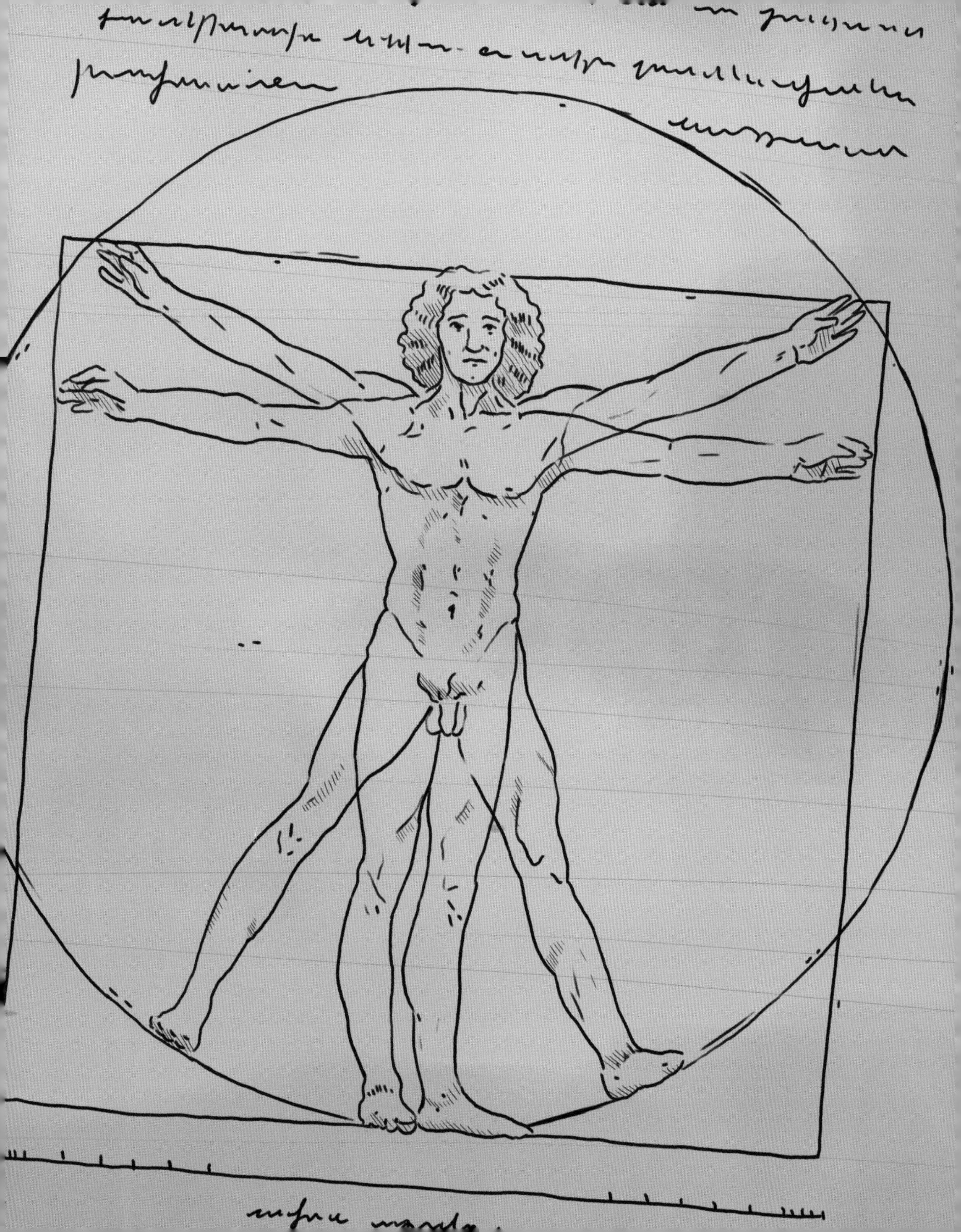

In 1495 I started work on a mural of "The Last Supper" in the refectory of the Santa Maria delle Grazie monastery. It was commissioned by the Duke of Milan, Ludovico Sforza.

The painting took me three years to complete and captures the moment when Jesus gathered his twelve apostles and says that one of them would soon betray him.

The French army invaded Milan in 1499. King Louis XII was determined to press his claim to the throne and the Sforza family was forced to flee. I also escaped as the fighting raged, making my way back to the relative safety of Florence.

During my time in Florence, I painted several portraits. The only one that survived is titled "Mona Lisa" and it was created around 1503. Over the years there has been much speculation about who the lady in the picture is. I will always keep her identity a secret, along with the reason for her half-smile. "Mona Lisa" has become probably the world's most famous painting.

In 1506 I moved back to Milan before finally settling in the Château of Clos Lucé, near Amboise in France, in 1517. This was at the invitation of the French king Francis I, who granted me the grand title of "Premier Painter and Engineer and Architect to the King". The beautiful Château was the perfect place for me to live out the rest of my life in peace and quiet. I rarely painted anymore.

Throughout my life I wrote about and drew on many subjects, from geology and anatomy to flight and gravity. Quite the inventor, I sketched a machine that resembles what we now call a bicycle, long before one was actually built.

I loved to study the flight of birds and the physiology of bats, and I often created plans for flying machines that look similar to the hang gliders and helicopters of today.

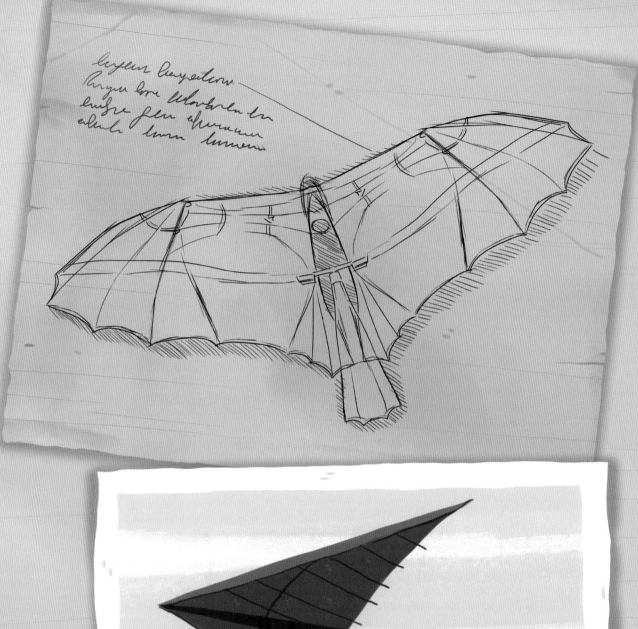

Perhaps because I had such a variety of interests, often I didn't complete my work, or I destroyed it because it wasn't quite as I wanted it. I did, however, fill notebook after notebook with my plans and ideas - though these can be quite hard for anyone but me to read, due to what some people call my left-handed "mirror script": I wrote the   letters as if they were reflected by a mirror!

I have become known as an artist-engineer, because I use scientific research to create my drawings and paintings. I tried to gain a deeper understanding of the workings of the human body, in order to make sure my work was as accurate as possible. Throughout my life I never stopped learning and exploring.

Leonardo da Vinci is born on 15th April in a small town in Tuscany.

Da Vinci becomes an independent master.

1452

1478

1466

He begins an apprenticeship with Andrea del Verrocchio in Florence.

He moves to Milan and works for the ruling family, the Sforzas.

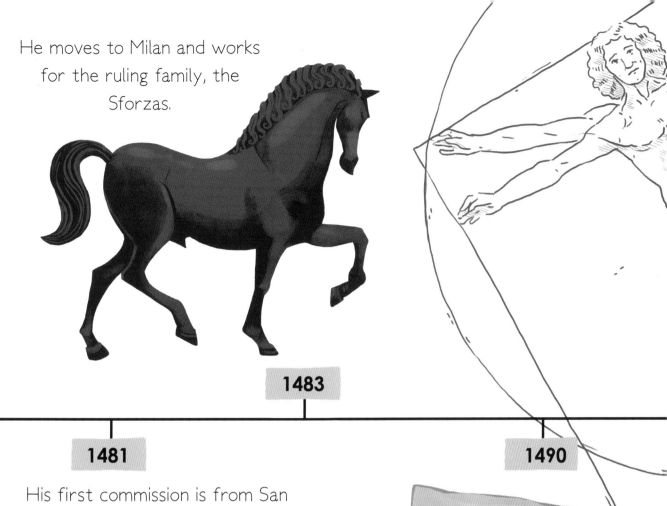

1483

1481

His first commission is from San Donato monastery in Florence, but the painting is left unfinished.

1490

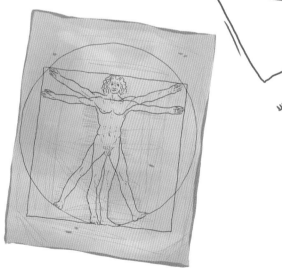

Da Vinci sketches the "Vitruvian Man".

Commissioned by the Duke of Milan, Ludovico Sforza, Da Vinci paints a mural of "The Last Supper".

He paints the portrait called "Mona Lisa".

1495

1503

1499

When the French army invaded Milan, Da Vinci escapes to the safety of Florence.

Da Vinci moves to France and is granted the title of "Premier Painter and Engineer and Architect to the King".

1517

1506

1519

Da Vinci dies, aged 67.

He returns to Milan and begins to teach a group of students.

QUESTIONS

Q1. Which famous sculptor and painter did
Da Vinci apprentice for?

Q2. Which hand did Da Vinci often choose to paint with?

Q3. What was Da Vinci's first commissioned work called?

Q4. Which ruling family did
Da Vinci work for in Milan?

Q5. Da Vinci believed which organ was
the most important in the human body?

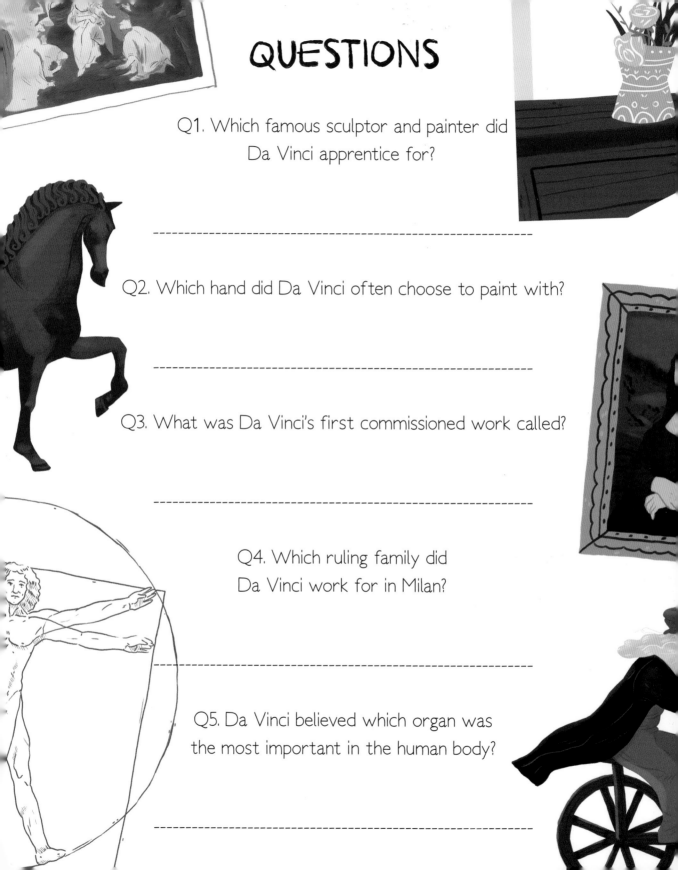

Q6. What is Da Vinci's sketch of a man with arms outstretched called?

Q7. How many years did it take Da Vinci to complete "The Last Supper"?

Q8. What grand title did French king Francis I grant Da Vinci?

Q9. Which is probably Da Vinci's most famous painting?

Q10. In what year did Da Vinci die?

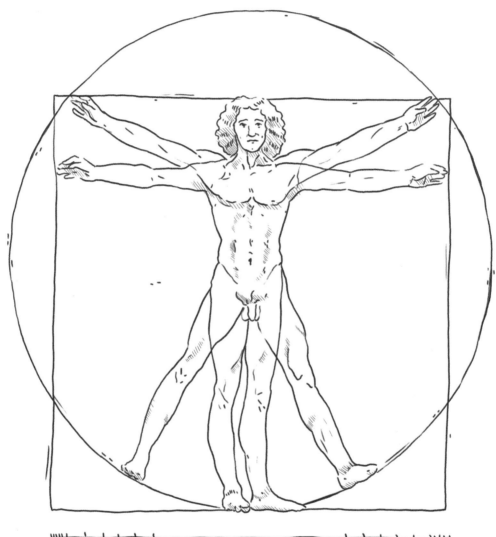

ANSWERS

A1. Andrea del Verrocchio.

A2. His left hand.

A3. "The Adoration of the Magi".

A4. The Sforza family.

A5. The eyes.

A6. "Vitruvian Man".

A7. Three years.

A8. "Premier Painter and Engineer and Architect to the King".

A9. "Mona Lisa".

A10. 1519.

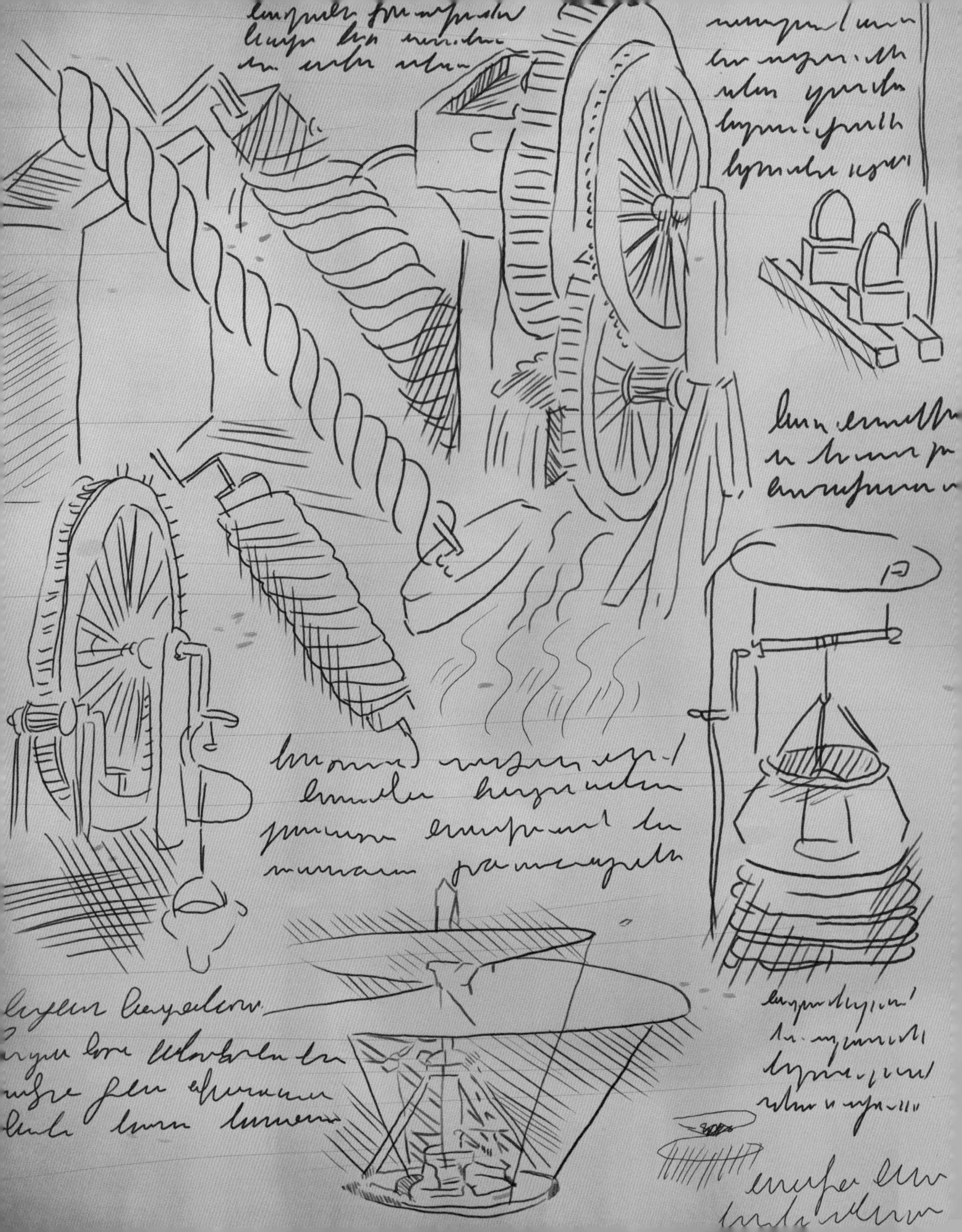